MW01224811
UBS

SAMMY SOSA

RICHARD J. BRENNER

BEECH TREE • NEW YORK
AN EAST END PUBLISHING BOOK

Sox

Sammy Sosa has taken a remarkable journey, from a childhood rooted in aching poverty to a full and rich life as a baseball superstar and humanitarian.

Although Sammy struggled early in his career, he emerged as one of the game's top sluggers in 1998, smashing a major-league–record 20 home runs in June and 66 overall, the second highest one-season total in big league history.

Franklin

Sammy was born November 12, 1968, in San Pedro de Macorís, a dusty, sunbaked, seaside town in the Dominican Republic, a Caribbean country that occupies the eastern two thirds of Hispaniola, the island it shares with Haiti.

The Dominican Republic is a Spanish-speaking nation that is located only 670 miles southeast of Florida, but a whole world away in terms of its economic development and the opportunities that are available to its people.

Sammy grew up even poorer than most of the people in his poverty-scarred country. His mother, Lucrecia, who was widowed when Sammy was only seven, did the best she could to support her seven children by working as a maid.

But life was very hard for the family, who lived in two rooms of a converted hospital, so Sammy did what he could to help by selling oranges and shining shoes in the town square.

CUBS

When Sammy had time, he played baseball, using a cardboard milk carton as his first mitt because he couldn't afford a real fielder's glove. Although he didn't start playing organized baseball until he was 14, by the time he was 16, Sammy had attracted the attention of major-league scouts, including Omar Minaya, who signed Sammy to a contract for the Texas Rangers.

Reaching for the big leagues wasn't just a dream for Sammy, but a way of avoiding the nightmare of a lifetime teetering on the edge of poverty.

"If it wasn't baseball, it would mean *trying* to find work in a factory, *trying* to make a living," said Sammy, who used that fear to fuel his ambition.

"From the first time I saw him, he set himself apart with his aggressiveness and his drive," said Sandy Johnson, who was the director of scouting for the Rangers when Sammy arrived in 1986. "He had this fire in his eyes. He was like a young colt out of control. But he was so determined to make it that you couldn't help but notice him."

SS

When Sammy arrived in the United States he was only 17, spoke almost no English, and was so scrawny that coaches thought he was malnourished.

Despite those disadvantages and his limited baseball experience, Sammy steadily climbed the rungs of the Rangers' minor-league ladder and earned a promotion to the Big Team in Arlington early in the 1989 season.

During what turned into a 25-game audition, Sammy clipped Roger Clemens for his first major-league home run, but he spent most of his other swings chasing pitches in distant zip codes. The Rangers quickly grew impatient watching their free-swinging outfielder wave at pitches in the dirt, and traded him to the Chicago White Sox.

Two years later, after seeing him strike out more often than he made contact, the White Sox also gave up on Sammy, and dealt him to the Chicago Cubs.

CUBS

NIKE
21

52

When Sammy came to the Cubs for the 1992 season, he was carrying the baggage of a .228 career batting average and a reputation as a careless and unschooled player who lacked basic baseball skills.

"You could see he had great physical talent, but he didn't know how to play the game," said Cubs first baseman and team leader Mark Grace, after watching Sammy position himself in the same spot for Big Fly swatters and singles hitters. "He played Barry Bonds and Rafael Belliard the same."

Sammy finally started progressing as a player in 1993, finishing the season as the first player in Cubs history to hit 30 homers and steal 30 bases. And he continued his development over the course of the next four seasons, averaging slightly more than 34 homers and 100 RBIs per season, while earning a spot on the 1995 National League All-Star team.

But nothing that Sammy had done prepared anyone for what he was about to accomplish.

SOSA
21

Ironically, Sammy got off to a slow start in 1998, hitting only nine home runs through the first eight weeks of the season. But over the following five weeks, he started hitting dingers like they were One-A-Day vitamins. From May 25 through June 30, Sammy slammed 24 homers, including 20 in the month of June, two more than any other player had ever hit in any month of any season.

"I've seen a lot of things in this game, but I've never seen anything like this," said Mark Grace.

With 33 dingers under his belt, Sammy was suddenly running with the Big Dogs, trailing only Ken Griffey, Jr., who had tagged 35, and major-league leader Mark McGwire, who had bagged 37.

"Sammy's scary right now," said Philadelphia Phillies catcher Mark Parent. "He doesn't chase pitches like he used to, and he makes pitchers pay for their mistakes. That's the big thing for all good hitters, like Mac and Junior, they don't swing at a lot of bad pitches, and they hammer most of the mistakes."

ICE MOUNTAIN

The midseason totals put up by Big Mac, Junior, and Sammy created a current of excitement throughout the world of baseball. Fans everywhere began talking about the pursuit of Roger Maris's record of 61 homers in a season. And while Griffey's pace soon slowed, the continued run at the record by Big Mac and Sammy became the sports story of the decade.

"I'm no Roger Maris," claimed Sammy. "I'm no Mark McGwire. He's the man. Me, I'm just another kid on the block having a pretty good season."

CUBS
21

By the end of August, it was clear that Sammy was having a *spectacular* season. He was leading the National League in RBIs and had already hammered 53 homers, matching McGwire dinger for dinger. "It's just a blast," said Kerry Wood, the Cubs' rookie pitching sensation. "Sammy puts on a show every day."

"I'm not thinking about the home run record," insisted Sammy, who celebrated each Big Fly by blowing kisses to his mother and giving a victory sign in honor of Harry Caray, the former Cubs announcer who had died during spring training. "I'm just focusing on helping my team make the playoffs."

Sammy had an on-field view of McGwire's record-breaking 62d homer that erased the record that had stood for 37 years. He trotted in from right field to embrace his friendly rival, and five days later tied him at 62, setting off a four-minute standing ovation at Chicago's Wrigley Field. "Unbelievable," said Sammy about number 62. "It was something that I can't even believe I was doing."

Sammy's historic home run also touched off a celebration throughout the Windy City and in the Dominican Republic, where his adoring fans danced in the streets, chanting *"Sesenta y dos, sesenta y dos"*—sixty-two, sixty-two.

Sammy ended the season with 66 home runs, four behind McGwire, but second to no one in what he had accomplished during the 1998 season. He not only posted the second-highest home run total in major-league history, he also racked up 158 RBIs, the fourth-highest total in National League history, led the Cubs into the playoffs, and was named the league's MVP.

"It's been a beautiful year," said Sammy, speaking about Mac and himself and the joy that they had brought back to baseball. "No one is going to forget 1998."

Photo Credits: The photo on the front and back covers was taken by **Jonathan Daniel,** as were the photos on pages 26 and 32. The photo on page 24 was taken by **Vincent Laforet**, and was supplied by ALLSPORT, USA. The photo on page 2 was supplied by SPORTSCHROME, as was the centerfold, which was taken by **Rob Tringali, Jr.** All of the remaining photos were taken by **Tony Inzerillo**.

Published by Beech Tree Books, a division of William Morrow and Company, Inc.
1350 Avenue of the Americas, New York, NY 10019
www.williammorrow.com

Printed in the United States of America.

First Beech Tree Edition, 1999
ISBN 0-688-17084-6

10 9 8 7 6 5 4 3 2 1

CUBS